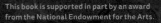

Text and illustrations
©2018 Linda Bondestam
Published in English by
arrangement with Rights & Brands
Translation ©2021 Galit Hasan-Rokem

First published as *God natt på jorden*
by Förlaget, Helsinki, 2018 and
Berghs Förlag, Stockholm, 2018

First Restless Books hardcover
edition April 2021

Hardcover ISBN: 9781632062864
Library of Congress Control Number:
2020945879

Cover design by Jonathan Yamakami
Cover illustration by Linda Bondestam

Printed in Italy
1 3 5 7 9 10 8 6 4 2

This book is supported in part by an award
from the National Endowment for the Arts.

This book is made possible by the New York State
Council on the Arts with the support of Governor
Andrew M. Cuomo and the New York State Legislature.

This work has been published with the financial
assistance of FILI – Finnish Literature Exchange.

NEW YORK
STATE OF OPPORTUNITY | Council on
the Arts

FILI FINNISH
LITERATURE
EXCHANGE

Restless Books, Inc.
232 3rd Street, Suite A101
Brooklyn, NY 11215

www.restlessbooks.org
publisher@restlessbooks.org

GOOD NIGHT, EARTH

Linda Bondestam

TRANSLATED FROM THE SWEDISH
BY GALIT HASAN-ROKEM

RESTLESS BOOKS
BROOKLYN, NEW YORK

LITTLE CHIMP SHOULD BE ASLEEP BY NOW.
MAMA HAS SUNG AND PLAYED 73 SONGS
ON HER UKULELE.

THE AXOLOTL IS SO, SO TIRED.

HE SWALLOWS A GULP OF FRESH WATER AND

READS HIS FAVORITE BOOK. THEN HE YAWNS A BIG YAWN.

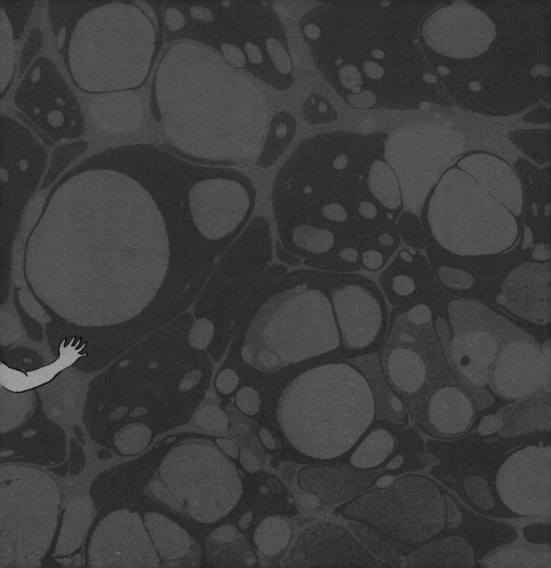

LOOK, LOOK, THERE ARE THE CATS! THEY DRINK A SIP OF MILK AND WASH THEIR WHISKERS. AND THEN IT'S BEDTIME.

GOOD NIGHT, EVERYBODY!

WHO ARE THEY? MAYBE MERRY CATS ON THE SAVANNA?
OH NO, IT'S THE MEERKAT FAMILY RELAXING A BIT
WITH SOME EVENING STRETCHES.

NOW THEY CRAWL HOME TO THEIR CAVES, SO COZY!

SLEEP TIGHT, MEERKAT FAMILY!

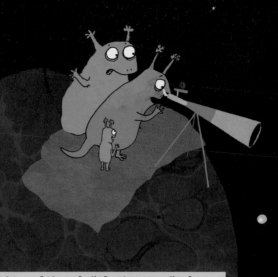

WHO HAS MADE A BED FOR HERSELF ON THE ROOF?

IT'S THE SNEAKY TARSIER!

WILL SHE SLEEP TIGHT?

OH NO, SHE IS GOING TO SNEAK
AROUND ALL NIGHT!

IN THIS FAMILY NO ONE WANTS TO GO TO SLEEP.

"JUMP INTO YOUR BEDS,"

PAPA KIWI HOLLERS.

BUT NO! HE HAS TO PLAY FLYING RAISINS FOR HOURS.

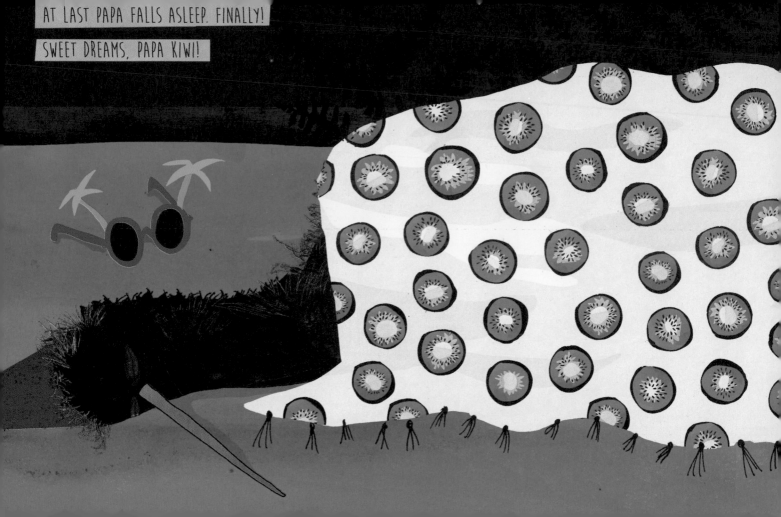

AT LAST PAPA FALLS ASLEEP. FINALLY!

SWEET DREAMS, PAPA KIWI!

LOOK THERE, IN THE LEAVES! A LITTLE SLOTH IN A HAMMOCK!

SHHH! BOTH SHE AND THE HAMMOCK ARE ASLEEP, AS USUAL.

WHAT'S THE MATTER WITH THE TREES?
THEY BOW THEIR BRANCHES AND TOSS
THEIR LEAFY CLOTHES INTO THE WIND.

PAJAMAS AND FLUFFY BLANKET, ALL IN ONE.
SWEET DREAMS TO YOU, NATURE!

SWEETIE PIE FALLS ASLEEP SO SWEETLY, SO NICELY, AFTER MAMA HAS SUNG AND PLAYED 73 SONGS ON HER UKULELE, AFTER PAPA HAS SERVED UP A SIP OF MILK, WASHED THEIR WHISKERS, AND READ THEIR FAVORITE BOOKS, AND THEY HAVE ALL PLAYED FLYING RAISINS AND RELAXED WITH SOME EVENING STRETCHES.

ALL RIGHT, NOW SWEETIE PIE CAN SLEEP TIGHT TOO!

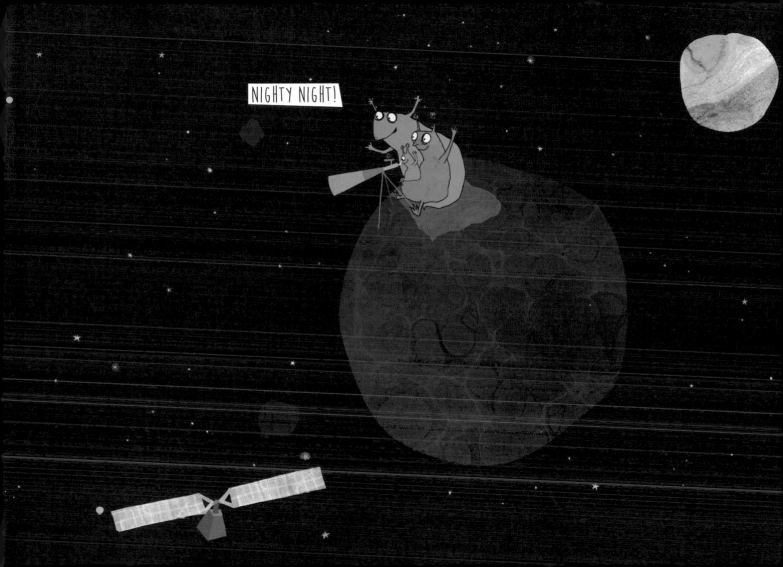

NOW THE SUN IS UP—WHAT A SIGHT.
GOOD MORNING, EARTH!
IT SEEMS TO BE SUPPERTIME FOR THE OWL FAMILY.
YAWN!

HEY, IT'S DAY!

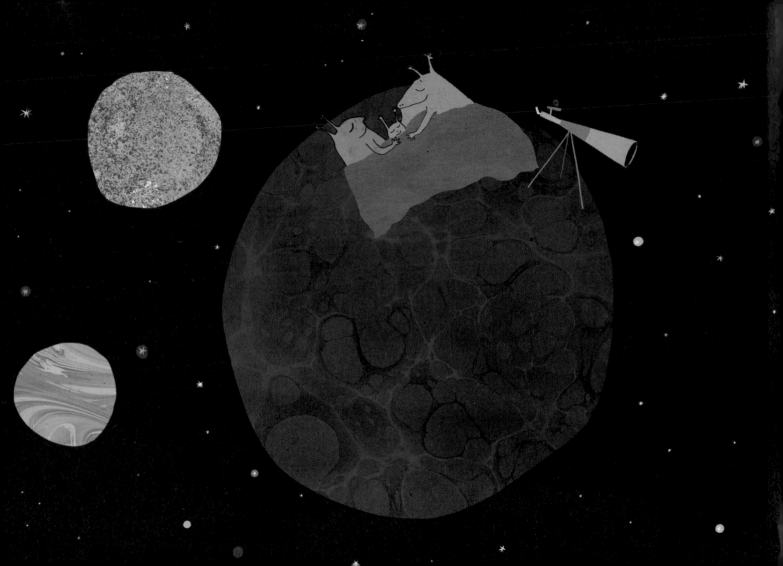

ABOUT THE AUTHOR

Linda Bondestam is an illustrator based in Helsinki. A graduate of Kingston University in London, she has illustrated dozens of children's books that have been translated into more than ten languages. One of the most celebrated illustrators in the Nordic countries, Linda was awarded the Snöbollen for Swedish Picture Book of the Year in 2016 and the Nordic Council Children and Young People's Literature Prize in 2017 for *Djur som ingen sett utom vi* (Animals that no one has seen except us). She was also nominated for the August Prize in 2020 for *Mitt bottenliv* (My life at the bottom) and is a six-time ALMA nominee, among various other awards. *Good Night, Earth* is her authorial debut.

ABOUT THE TRANSLATOR

Galit Hasan-Rokem is a folklore scholar, translator, and Professor Emerita in the Department of Hebrew Literature at the Hebrew University of Jerusalem. She continues to conduct research, supervise graduate students, and translate poetry, mainly from the Swedish into Hebrew. She is the author of many books and articles and a published poet, as well as the founding editorial board member and cultural editor of *Palestine-Israel Journal*, the coeditor of *Jerusalem Studies in Jewish Folklore*, and the associate editor of *Proverbium*.

ABOUT YONDER

Yonder is an imprint from Restless Books devoted to bringing the wealth of great stories from around the globe to English-reading children, middle graders, and young adults. Books from other countries, cultures, viewpoints, and storytelling traditions can open up a universe of possibility, and the wider our view, the more powerfully books enrich and expand us. In an increasingly complex, globalized world, stories are potent vehicles of empathy. We believe it is essential to teach our kids to place themselves in the shoes of others beyond their communities, and instill in them a lifelong curiosity about the world and their place in it. Through publishing a diverse array of transporting stories, Yonder nurtures the next generation of savvy global citizens and lifelong readers.